W9-AHR-265

BEWARE the PHARAOH'S TOMB!

by Michael Teitelbaum

illustrated by Jose Emroca Flores

New York, New York

Credits
Cover: © Jose Ignacio Soto/Shutterstock, ©Anton_Ivanov/Shutterstock, © PRILL/Shutterstock, and © Bojan Pavlukovic/Shutterstock.

Publisher: Kenn Goin
Editorial Director: Natalie Lunis
Creative Director: Spencer Brinker
Text produced by Scout Books & Media Inc.

Library of Congress Cataloging-in-Publication Data in process at time of publication (2016)
Library of Congress Control Number: 2015020029
ISBN-13: 978-1-62724-810-5

For more information, write to Bearport Publishing Company, Inc., 45 West 21st Street, Suite 3B, New York, New York 10010.
Printed in the United States of America.

10 9 8 7 6 5 4 3 2 1

Contents

CHAPTER 1

Oh No, a Substitute Teacher!

Sam and his fifth-grade classmates were thrilled. Their teacher, Mrs. Shirley, was going to take them on a field trip to the Natural History Museum. The class had been studying **ancient** Egypt, and the museum had a huge exhibit on the topic. The highlight of the exhibit was the **ruins** of an ancient Egyptian **temple**.

"This is going to be the coolest field trip ever!" Sam said to his best friend Elliot, as he pushed his thick brown hair out of his dark brown eyes.

"Especially for you," Elliot said. "You have been wild about ancient Egypt ever since you got that picture book in second grade." Elliot was several inches taller than Sam and had sandy blond hair and blue eyes.

The classroom door suddenly swung open and slammed into the wall, snapping everyone in the room to attention. In walked a tall man with very long legs, white hair, and deep, piercing eyes. He wore a long coat that went all the way down to his ankles. The coat had streaks of brightly colored fabric and shiny gold buttons.

"My name is Mr. Farrow," he said in a low, commanding voice. "I am your substitute teacher for the day."

Sam leaned over to Elliot. "Oh, no!" he whispered. "This means no field trip."

Mr. Farrow whipped around to face Sam. "Actually, young man, it means nothing of the kind," he said. His eyes focused right on Sam. "What is your name?"

"Sam," he replied **sheepishly**.

"Well, Sam, today we are all going to Egypt," Mr. Farrow said in his powerful voice.

Sam sighed in relief, exchanging a quick high five with Elliot.

Mr. Farrow walked to the board and wrote his name—first in English and then as an Egyptian **hieroglyph**, or drawing.

Sam was thrilled. He had studied Egyptian hieroglyphs ever since he first saw one in a book. He could even read some of them. But he'd never seen a hieroglyph like the one on the board. He drew a copy of it in his notebook. Then he raised his hand.

"Did you create that hieroglyph, Mr. Farrow?" he asked.

"Yes, Sam," the teacher replied. "It's one of a kind. I lived in Egypt a number of years ago. I know a great deal about Egyptian history, especially when it comes to reading and creating hieroglyphs."

Sam leaned over to Elliot again. "This guy is awesome," he whispered, even more softly than before, so Mr. Farrow wouldn't hear.

Mr. Farrow smiled. "Please line up and pick a travel partner for the trip," he said.

Naturally, Sam chose Elliot to be his travel partner. The two friends headed to the front of the line. Sam could hardly contain his excitement.

CHAPTER 2

The Field Trip Is On

On the bus ride to the museum, Mr. Farrow talked to the class about life in ancient Egypt.

"I'm sure you've learned about the process by which **mummies** are created," he began. "But did you know that some **Pharaohs** were buried with their mummified cats?"

A mixed chorus of "Cool!" and "Gross!" filled the bus.

"Here's something you may not have read in your history books," Mr. Farrow continued. "If a Pharaoh didn't have a child, he could choose another person to be his **heir**."

Sam raised his hand. "What was it like being a kid in ancient Egypt?" he asked. "We haven't studied that yet."

"Excellent question, Sam," Mr. Farrow said. "If the Pharaoh had children, they led a life of wealth, waited upon by servants and taught by private tutors. Most other children, however, worked endless hours in the hot sun, building **pyramids**."

"I'd hate to be one of those kids," said a girl who was sitting near Sam.

Throughout the ride, Sam continued to ask questions. Mr. Farrow was an expert in Egyptian history, and Sam was not going to waste this chance to learn all he could. And Mr. Farrow seemed impressed by Sam's knowledge and **intellectual** curiosity.

Before Sam knew it, the bus turned into the museum parking lot. His great Egyptian adventure was about to begin!

As the students got off the bus, a tour guide named Sara greeted them.

"I want to welcome you to the Natural History Museum," she said. "I understand that your class has been studying ancient Egypt. Well, all I can say is that you are in for a treat! Now, please follow me."

Sara led Mr. Farrow and the class into the museum. Sam felt his excitement building as the exhibit came into view. The group stopped at a display of early tools used by Egyptians. Pulling out his notebook, Sam started sketching pictures of some of the tools.

"I've only read about these," he said to himself. "But to see actual tools from that time . . . Wow!"

The next exhibit contained a model of a half-built pyramid. It also showed tiny figures hauling large stones toward the unfinished structure. Again, Sam pulled out his notebook.

Sam was so busy looking and sketching, he didn't notice that his class had moved on. He was now alone.

He looked around but saw no one. Sam wandered down a long empty hallway. "Where am I?" he wondered aloud. "How am I going to find the class?"

At the end of the hallway, Sam stepped into a dimly lit room in another part of the museum. He looked up and froze. There stood a man holding an ax over his head.

CHAPTER 3
Trapped!

"Stop!" Sam shrieked, throwing his hands up and backing away. He crashed into a wall and then realized that the man he had seen was just a suit of **armor** on display.

"Nice going, Sam," he mumbled to himself. "You'd better find the class."

He stepped out of the room and felt something grab his shoulder.

"Aaahhh!" Sam screamed. *What could it be? A mummy come to life? A poisonous Egyptian snake?*

"It's all right, Sam," said Mr. Farrow, holding on to Sam's shoulder. "I noticed you weren't with the class, so I went looking for you. I don't want you to miss any more of the tour."

Sam exhaled. "I'm sorry," he said. "Thanks for finding me."

Mr. Farrow led Sam back to the group, where he met up with Elliot.

"Where were you?" asked Elliot.

"I kind of got lost," Sam explained.

"Please stay with the group," said Sara. "We were concerned."

"Yeah, concerned that we'd have to miss some of the tour because of you," said a boy in the class, rolling his eyes.

"Sorry," Sam said again.

Sara and Mr. Farrow led the group to the next exhibit.

"Check this out," said Elliot. He pointed to a sandstone wall covered with Egyptian hieroglyphs.

"Wow!" said Sam, stepping up to the wall. He looked over the various ancient hieroglyphs, trying to see if he could **interpret** them. Then he pointed to one and gasped. "This looks just like the hieroglyph Mr. Farrow drew on the board this morning—the one he said he created himself."

Sam grabbed his notebook and flipped to the page where he had sketched Mr. Farrow's hieroglyph. He held it up next to the one on the sandstone.

"It's the same," he said. "How is that possible?"

"That *is* weird," said Elliot.

Sam glanced down at his notebook, then back up at the wall. He reached out and touched the hieroglyph on the wall, tracing its lines with his finger.

"This is *really* strange," said Sam. "This hieroglyph feels warm." He pulled his hand away just as Sara stepped up to them.

"Boys, I'm going to have to ask you to keep up with the class," she said. "Please come this way."

Sam and Elliot followed Sara into a large room, where Mr. Farrow and the rest of the class were waiting.

"This is the Discovery Center," Sara said. "It's the one place where it's okay to look at *and* touch certain items. Let's begin in the mummy section."

Sam entered an area filled with models of mummies in tall open cases. Examples of tools used to create mummies were laid out on nearby tables. He picked up a wooden tool with a curved hook.

"Do you know what that tool was used for, Sam?" Mr. Farrow asked.

"It was used to pull a dead person's brain out of his head through the nose," he replied.

"Yuck," said several of Sam's classmates.

"Correct," said Mr. Farrow.

"Next, we'll look at what happened to bodies after they were mummified," said Sara. She led the class over to a raised platform on which sat a **reproduction** of a **sarcophagus**.

"Who wants to experience what it would be like to be inside a sarcophagus?" Sara asked.

"Not me! Not me!" exclaimed some students.

Elliot's hand shot up. "Me!" he said.

Sara gestured to the platform. Elliot stepped up and into the open sarcophagus. Then Sara closed the lid on him. After about thirty seconds, Elliot pushed it open.

"Wow!" Elliot said as he stepped out and high-fived Sam. "How long was I in there for? It felt like a while."

"Only a few seconds," Mr. Farrow said. "Imagine spending an **eternity** in one of these as an ancient Egyptian mummy. Your turn, Sam."

Sam wondered why he was next, since he hadn't volunteered. But he stepped up onto the platform and into the sarcophagus.

"Ready?" Sara asked.

Sam nodded. The lid slowly closed. All light gradually faded. Sam found himself in total darkness.

Sam felt strange being inside this box with absolutely no light. The thought of spending forever inside the sarcophagus made him nervous. His heart started to beat a little faster. Sweat broke out on his forehead.

Time to get out of here, Sam thought. He pushed on the lid, but it didn't **budge**. He pushed harder. Still, it didn't open.

"Hey! Let me out of here!" Sam shouted. "I'm trapped!"

CHAPTER 4
The Great Temple

Sam pounded on the inside of the lid. "Help!" he cried. "Let me out!"

He shoved hard but couldn't get it to budge. In his growing panic, he thought of Mr. Farrow's words: *Imagine spending an eternity in one of these.*

All of a sudden, the lid popped open. Sam was blinded by a sudden flood of light. Sara reached in and helped him out of the sarcophagus.

"Are you all right?" she asked, helping Sam step off the platform.

His eyes adjusted to the light, and his heart slowed down. "What happened?" he asked.

"The lid must have gotten stuck," Sara said. "I'm so sorry."

"I'm okay," Sam said. He looked around for Mr. Farrow to tell him what it felt like to be trapped inside a sarcophagus. But Mr. Farrow was no longer there. *Where did he go?* thought Sam.

"Okay, everyone, it's time for the best part of the tour," said Sara. "Follow me into the Great Temple. But remember, this is a 'No Touch' area. Look, but please do not touch anything."

Sam followed his classmates down a hallway. Once again, he lagged behind, pausing to look carefully at every display he passed. He walked by a dark room and spotted Mr. Farrow quietly standing in front of a glass display case. The case contained a full Pharaoh's costume on a **mannequin** and a sign that read: "Costume of the Pharaoh Menkaura."

Sam wanted to rejoin his classmates, but his curiosity got the better of him. He walked up to Mr. Farrow.

COSTUME OF THE
PHARAOH
MENKAURA

"Mr. Farrow," said Sam, wondering why the teacher had stepped away from the tour. "Why are you looking at that costume so closely?"

"It is somewhat familiar to me, Sam," Mr. Farrow replied. "I recall seeing one like it once, a very long time ago. It is a special costume, worn by the Pharaoh only when he chose his heir. It's particularly beautiful, don't you think, Sam?"

"Yes, it's really beautiful," said Sam. The costume was made of silken fabric, shining gold, and many jewels. A golden headpiece rested on the mannequin's head. In the center of the headpiece Sam noticed a hieroglyph. Leaning in close to the display, Sam took a good look at the hieroglyph. His eyes opened wide. Once again, he recognized it. It was the symbol Mr. Farrow had drawn on the board—the symbol for his name!

"Mr. Farrow, why is this hieroglyph here?" Sam asked, turning toward the teacher. But Mr. Farrow was gone. Sam was standing alone in front of the display.

"Mr. Farrow?" he called, but got no reply.

Sam rushed from the room to catch up to his classmates at the Great Temple.

When Sam turned a corner, he spotted some kids from his group entering a room. He caught up to them and stepped into the Great Temple. It felt as if he had been sent back in time. The temple was made of huge stone blocks set on either side of narrow passageways. The walls were covered with carvings, paintings, and hieroglyphic symbols.

Sam could hear Sara's voice coming from down one of the passageways. He hurried along, hoping to join the group before Sara noticed he was missing again.

As Sam walked deeper into the temple, the ceiling got higher and the passageway was lined with tall stone columns. Sara's voice grew louder with each step Sam took. He picked up his pace—then something leaped out from behind a column!

Sam screamed. He flung his arms out in front of him, crashing into the wall in the process.

"Gotcha!" shouted Elliot, laughing.

"You really scared me," said Sam, catching his breath.

Footsteps pounded down the stone hallway. Sam and Elliot backed away.

"Someone's coming!" Sam cried.

Sara appeared, rushing toward them.

"I heard a scream," she said, out of breath. "Is everyone all right?"

"Yes, sorry," said Elliot. "Just a little joke."

"I'll ask you again to please stay with your classmates," said Sara. "I don't know where your teacher has gone—he should be looking after you." Sara led the boys into the center of the temple.

CHAPTER 5 A Real Nightmare

"Egyptian temples were made up of many chambers," Sara said. "This was the central chamber where all the temple's priests gathered each morning."

"But the most special and important chamber in the temple was the inner **sanctuary**," Sara continued, gesturing toward a dark hallway. "Located deep in the innermost part of the temple, it was a place that only the Pharaoh and his high priests were allowed to enter. Our tour today will end there, but first follow me to the Sun **Shrine**. This way, please."

Sara led the group down a passageway leading in the opposite direction from the inner sanctuary. Sam lingered for a moment. As he was about to follow the group, he heard a strange sound coming from the dark hallway. Curious, he snuck away again and started toward the inner sanctuary.

Sam walked slowly to the end of the dark corridor. There, he entered the sanctuary, which glowed with a soft light. He looked around, but no one was there.

The inner sanctuary had a tall ceiling that was painted gold. The room was **sparse**, holding just several stone benches and a large **altar**. Stepping up to the altar, Sam's eyes were drawn to a hieroglyph—*the* hieroglyph he had seen throughout the museum. Mr. Farrow's hieroglyph! *How could this be?* Sam thought.

Sam heard the sound of footsteps approaching.

"Nice try, Elliot," he said. "But you're not going to scare me again."

"Sam," whispered a voice.

Out of the corner of his eye, Sam saw someone moving in the shadows. Then the movement stopped.

Sam felt a hand on his arm. His heart started to race. He spun around.

"Not funny, Elli—" he began, stopping suddenly. A man dressed in a Pharaoh's costume stood close beside him. Sam recognized the costume—it was the one from the display case. Trembling, he looked up into the Pharaoh's face.

"Mr. Farrow!" he said, relieved but confused. "What are you doing here? Why are you wearing that?"

"I am not who you think I am, Sam," said Mr. Farrow. "For you see, I am not Mr. Farrow."

"Wh-who are you?" Sam stammered.

"I am Pharaoh Menkaura, and this is my temple," he answered in a deep voice. "I am here to find an heir. Now that I have found one, it is time for me to go home. Will you help me, Sam?" he asked. "Only when we touch the hieroglyph together can I go home."

Mr. Farrow reached for Sam's hand, and guided it to the hieroglyph on the altar. Then Mr. Farrow placed his own hand on the hieroglyph.

Sam felt the wall get warm and then hotter and hotter. The heat burned his hand. His vision blurred. Then everything went black.

Out of nowhere, brilliant sunshine glared in Sam's eyes. He put his hand to his brow to block the sunlight and looked out at an **expanse** of desert before him. He squeezed his eyes shut, then opened them again. He was in a grand temple looking out at the huge pyramids in ancient Egypt. Sam had no idea how he had gotten here, but suddenly, he felt both scared and excited.

Pharaoh Menkaura put an arm around Sam's shoulder. "Beautiful, isn't it," he said. Then he stepped back to let Sam take it all in.

A tutor then rushed over to Sam. "Young Pharaoh, we must begin today's lessons," he said.

What is he talking about? Sam wondered.

The Pharaoh walked over to Sam and asked him, "What do you think, Sam?"

"This is so cool," Sam said, forgetting about the tutor for a moment. "The whole thing feels so real, the pyramid, the people. I can't wait to get back home and tell Elliot all about it."

"You misunderstand, Sam," said Pharaoh Menkaura, putting his arm around Sam once again. "*This* is your home now. And when I die, my great powers and responsibilities will be **bestowed** upon you. *You* will be the next Pharaoh of Egypt."

Sam felt the hot desert breeze against his skin, as a question raced through his mind. *Was the Pharaoh telling the truth?* If he was, Sam was ready to find out what his life would be like as the ruler of all of Egypt.

Sam turned to the tutor and said, "Yes, I'm ready for my lessons."

Beware the Pharaoh's Tomb!

1. Sam and his classmates were excited about going on a field trip. Where did they go and what did they see? Give examples from the story.

2. In Chapter 3, the students visit a room called the Discovery Center and learn about mummies. What is a mummy?

3. What is going on in the picture at right?

4. What is this symbol (see bottom picture) and what does it mean? Use examples from the story to explain.

5. In the story, Sam is sent to ancient Egypt. If you could be sent to another place and time, where would you want to go and why?

GLOSSARY

altar (AWL-tur) a table used for religious ceremonies

ancient (AYN-shuhnt) belonging to a time long ago

armor (AR-muhr) a protective metal covering worn by soldiers in battle

bestowed (bih-STOHD) given to

budge (BUHDJ) to cause to move

eternity (ih-TUR-nuh-tee) an unending period of time

expanse (ek-SPANSS) a large, open area

heir (AIR) someone who will inherit something

hieroglyph (*hye*-ur-uh-GLIF) an Egyptian symbol

intellectual (*in*-tuh-LEK-choo-uhl) thoughtful and smart

interpret (in-TUR-prit) to figure out what something means

mannequin (MAN-ih-kin) a life-size model of a human being

mummies (MUHM-eez) preserved dead bodies

Pharaohs (FAIR-ohz) ancient Egyptian kings

pyramids (PIHR-uh-midz) stone monuments

reproduction (*ree*-pruh-DUHK-shuhn) a copy

ruins (ROO-ihnz) the remains of something destroyed

sanctuary (SANGK-choo-ehr-ee) a sacred or holy place

sarcophagus (sahr-KOF-uh-*guhs*) a stone coffin

sheepishly (SHEE-pish-lee) in a shy manner

shrine (SHRINE) a building associated with holiness

sparse (SPAHRS) not crowded

temple (TEM-puhl) a building used for worship

ABOUT THE AUTHOR

Michael Teitelbaum is the author of more than 150 children's books, including young adult and middle-grade novels, tie-in novelizations, and picture books. His most recent books are *The Very Hungry Zombie: A Parody* and its sequel *The Very Thirsty Vampire: A Parody,* both created with illustrator Jon Apple. Michael and his wife, Sheleigah, live with two talkative cats in a farmhouse (as yet unhaunted) in upstate New York.

ABOUT THE ILLUSTRATOR

Jose Emroca Flores is an artist, illustrator, and designer who has worked on films, games, books, animations, galleries, and advertising. He is currently working as a freelance designer/illustrator based in Carlsbad, California.

When he is not creating art, you can find him surfing, traveling, riding his motorcycle, and spending time with his family and friends.